NORTH
POLE

13451 Wetmore Road
San Antonio, Texas 78247

ISBN 978-0-9795302-2-7
Library of Congress Control Number: 2007906348

This book is a work of fiction. Names, characters, places, and incidents are either products of the authors' imaginations, or are used fictitiously. Any resemblance to actual events or locales or persons, either living or dead, is entirely coincidental.

If you would like additional copies from the *Little Mike and Maddie* series of books, please visit:

www.CrumbGobbler.com

Little Mike and Maddie's
Christmas Book
Miriam Aronson
& Jeff Aronson
Illustrated By Jay Zephyr & Jeff Aronson

Little Mike and Maddie were happy dogs and loved to go on motorcycle adventures with Big Bob and Amy. They loved Christmas, too. There were so many fun things to do like picking out just the right tree at the Christmas tree farm.

"How about the orange one over there?" Amy said to Big Bob, pointing to a tree standing all by itself. It looked so lonely, and Little Mike and Maddie knew right away they had found their special tree.

After Supper, Big Bob, Amy, Little Mike and Maddie had lots of fun decorating the tree from top to bottom until it didn't look lonely at all anymore. Little Mike and Maddie had never Seen a more beautiful Christmas tree.

"Who wants to help bake cookies and wrap presents for the toy run?" Said Amy. Little Mike and Maddie were so excited about the motorcycle ride to collect gifts for the Children's Home. Soon Maddie was covered with flour. She loved to eat and she especially loved Christmas cookies. Little Mike loved cookies, too, but he liked to play most of all. He jumped into a big pile of bows and got one stuck on his head.

In the morning the house still smelled like cookies and the presents for the toy run were wrapped and ready to go. "It's cold outside, but not too cold for a motorcycle ride," Big Bob said as Amy slipped a fuzzy sweater over Little Mike's head.

Little Mike felt silly in his sweater. Maddie was lucky because she had lots of fur to keep her warm. They jumped into the sidecar next to Big Bob and Amy and "Vrumm, vrumm!" Off they went on the shiny red motorcycle to the toy run.

Little Mike and Maddie heard rumbling engines even before they got to the toy run. They loved the sound of motorcycles! People were smiling and laughing and everyone had gifts for the Children's Home.

Little Mike and Maddie were happy to see other dogs, too, and Little Mike wasn't the only one wearing a silly sweater. Some of the motorcycle riders wore costumes and looked so funny!

When a man dressed like one of Santa's elves gave the signal,
all the motorcycle riders fell into line and they were on their way.
More motorcycles joined them as they rode through town.
Traffic stopped and busy shoppers turned to watch and wave.
"We're on a toy run!" Little Mike barked to the family driving
by with a Christmas tree tied to the roof of their car.

AUNTIE'S INN
YE OLDE CANDY SHOP
WETM
LIBRA
TOY RUN

It was so much fun to ride along the winding twisty roads and down around the lake to see the ice-skaters. By the time they got back from the toy run, Little Mike and Maddie saw there were twice as many motorcycles as when they started.

"It's time for a Christmas party, Booger and Dog Breath!" Said Big Bob. Little Mike and Maddie were So happy to see a mountain of gifts for the Children's Home. They couldn't wait for Christmas Eve when they would go with Big Bob and Amy to surprise the kids with all the presents.

Soon everyone was eating cookies and singing Christmas carols. Little Mike and Maddie were so busy howling along that they didn't see the commotion at the door until they heard a loud "Ho, ho, ho! Merry Christmas!"

Santa Claus had arrived early for the Christmas parade! Little Mike and Maddie were glad he had stopped by their party to say hello. They ran outside to see Santa's sleigh and to meet Sidney, the road captain reindeer and the leader of Santa's newest reindeer team.

It didn't take long before Sidney and the rest of the reindeer were munching on lots of cookies. "It looks like the reindeer were hungry after your trip from the North Pole," Big Bob said to Santa Claus, who laughed and nodded his head.

A little later the reindeer weren't hungry at all because they had eaten way too many cookies. Their tummies ached and they couldn't move. Who was going to pull Santa's sleigh for the Christmas parade?

Luckily Sidney hadn't eaten as many cookies as the rest of the team. It was a rule that Santa's road captain reindeer always had to lead his sleigh. Little Mike looked at Maddie and Maddie looked at Little Mike. They had a terrific idea! Little Mike and Maddie gave Sidney a boost into the sidecar and they started barking so everyone would look their way.

"Ho, ho, ho!" said Santa Claus with a jolly laugh. "I think we'll be riding in the Christmas parade after all." Big Bob hooked the sleigh to the shiny red motorcycle while Little Mike, Maddie and Amy climbed in next to Santa. All the motorcycles from the toy run lined up behind them.

Off they went to join the parade, but first they stopped at the Children's Home to pick up the kids so they could ride along. The little girl with the pigtails sitting behind Big Bob smiled from ear to ear as they started up again with a booming "Vrumm, vrumm!"

"Merry Christmas, everyone!" Little Mike and Maddie barked to the people lining the streets to see Santa Claus and the Christmas parade.

It was a wonderful night, but all too soon the parade was over. Little Mike and Maddie were glad they would see the kids from the Children's Home again on Christmas Eve. They couldn't wait to surprise them with all the fun everyone had planned.

The next few days flew by with lots to do before Christmas Eve. There were more cookies to bake and carols to sing and ice skating with Big Bob and Amy.

Little Mike and Maddie couldn't believe how silly they both looked slipping and sliding on the ice.

At last it was Christmas Eve, and everyone from the toy run rode their motorcycles to the Children's Home. Little Mike and Maddie raced to greet the little girl with the pigtails who ran outside to give them a huge hug.

Little Mike and Maddie wagged their tails with excitement when they saw all the other kids, too. The children squealed with surprise and clapped their hands as the biggest tree they had ever seen was carried inside along with armloads of gifts.

Soon the tree was decorated, the tables filled with yummy things to eat, and the stockings hung by the chimney for Santa. Even the old shaggy dog that lived at the Children's Home got a special surprise from Little Mike and Maddie.

While the old dog wasn't looking, Little Mike laid his squeaky duck under the Christmas tree next to Maddie's green ball. It felt so good to give their favorite toys to their new friend and they hoped he liked them.

When the time came to say goodbye, Little Mike and Maddie were stuffed with Christmas goodies and their fur was rumpled from lots of hugs. The last thing they saw as they rode away was the old shaggy dog playing like a puppy with his new toys.

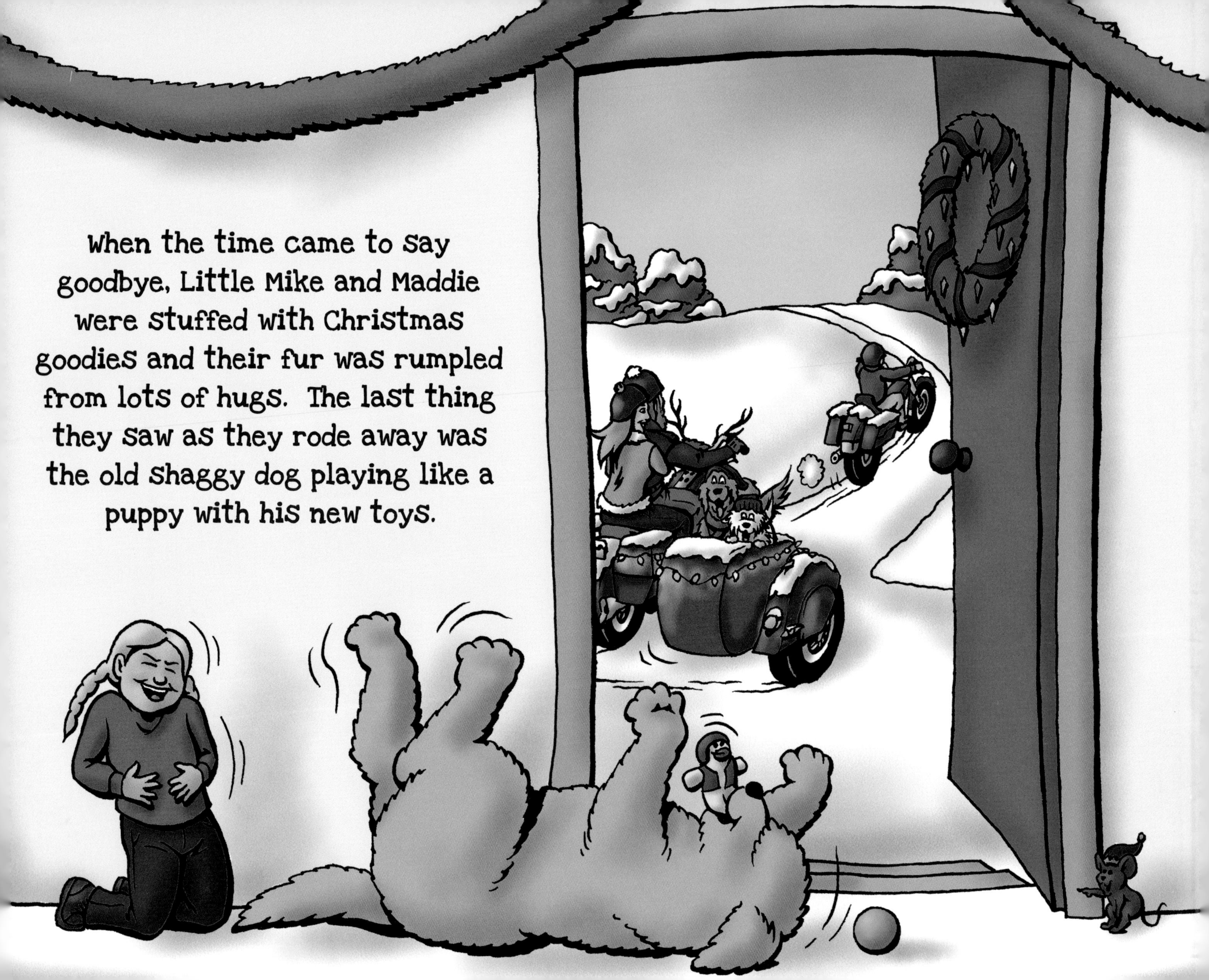

Back at home Little Mike and Maddie were getting sleepy, but they wanted to wait up for Santa Claus and to see Sidney again. "Here you go, my sweet peas," Amy said as she laid their bed on the floor. "We'll all wait for Santa together."

Little Mike tried to keep his eyes open, but he was getting sleepier and sleepier. Maddie was having trouble staying awake, too, until Amy set a plate of cookies on the table. "These cookies are for Santa," Amy said, "but you can have some when he gets here."

Maddie didn't mean to eat all of Santa's cookies, but she couldn't help herself. Everyone else had fallen asleep and the cookies smelled so good. She gobbled them down and then fell fast asleep, too. She didn't hear the reindeer hooves on the roof or see Santa smile at the empty cookie plate.

Little Mike and Maddie were sleeping so soundly that they didn't hear Santa Claus say, "Merry Christmas!" just before he went back up the chimney. They were dreaming about a shiny red motorcycle and another fun motorcycle adventure to come. Vrumm, vrumm . . . .

MERRY CHRISTMAS
Little Mike and Maddie's Christmas Book
Little Mike and Maddie's Christmas Book
CrumbGobbler Press

BIG BOB
TOY RUN